Time Traveling

By Catherine Lukas   Illustrated by Richard Torrey

Little Simon

New York   London   Toronto   Sydney   Singapore

Maya and Sam are best friends. Their buddy, Zach, runs the train museum. Today he greets them with a riddle.

"How can someone be in two different places at the same time?" says Zach.

"Impossible!" say Maya and Sam.

Zach smiles and blows his conductor's whistle. It is unlike any other whistle in the world. When they hear it toot, Maya and Sam know they are about to travel back in time!

"Wow!" says Maya. "Where are we, Zach? And *when*?"

"We're traveling west, clear across the United States," replies Zach. "And the year is 1884."

The train stops next to two kids waiting on the platform.

"Hi! We're Tobias and Jane," the two kids say. "Come with us! It's almost high noon!"

Inside the station everyone is looking at their pocket watches.

"They're waiting for the Western Union time signal," whispers Tobias. "They do this every Thursday to make sure their watches are right."

Suddenly the telegraph operator raises his hand. "High noon!" he calls out.

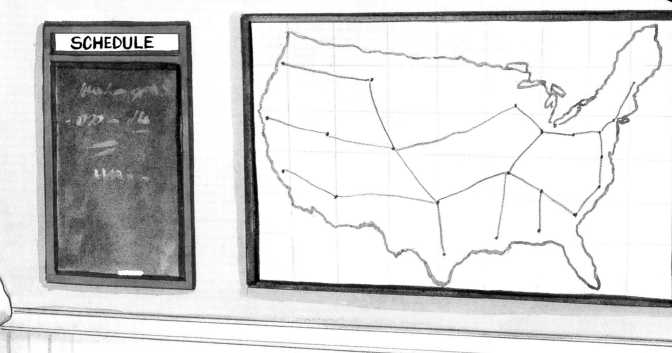

SCHEDULE

"People used to look at the position of the sun to tell time," Jane explains. "Every state went by a different time."

"Luckily, the railroad industry has standardized time all across the country," adds Zach. "Now there are four time zones: Pacific, Mountain, Central, and Eastern. Clocks within each time zone are set at the same time."

"This is our dad," says Jane proudly. "He's the station agent."

Their dad chuckles. "And I'm also the telegraph operator, the ticket seller, and the postmaster. Now that time zones have been established, my job is a lot easier. Before, people could wait for a train all day. Now trains run on actual schedules, and the entire country goes by railroad time!"

"It's nearly lunchtime," says their father. "Are you ready for a picnic?"

"Yes, sir!" shouts Jane, picking up the picnic basket.

After lunch Tobias points to the ground next to the picnic blanket. "This is the imaginary line separating Central time and Mountain time. We ate lunch at twelve thirty. But if we step over the line—"

"We can eat lunch all over again, because it's still just eleven thirty over there!" finishes Jane, laughing.

"Cool!" says Maya.

"Way cool!" says Sam. "But I don't think I could eat too much more."

Sam smiles slowly. "I think I've solved your riddle, Zach," he says. "If we stand here at twelve thirty, then step over the line and wait an hour, it will be twelve thirty over there, too. So we'd just have been in two different places at the same time!"

Zach nods. "That's right. You figured it out!"
Then he blows his magic whistle, and the three time
travelers find themselves back at the train museum.

"That was really fun, Zach, but look at the clock!" Sam says, and frowns. "My mom wants us home by noon—for lunch!"